This book belongs to:

_____

_____

_____

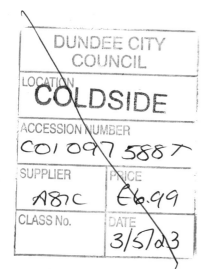
First published 2022 by Walker Books Ltd
87 Vauxhall Walk, London SE11 5HJ

2 4 6 8 10 9 7 5 3 1

This edition published 2023

Printed in China

British Library Cataloguing in Publication Data:
a catalogue record for this book is
available from the British Library.

ISBN 978-1-5295-0809-3

www.walker.co.uk

Maisy Goes on a Nature Walk

Lucy Cousins

WALKER BOOKS
AND SUBSIDIARIES
LONDON • BOSTON • SYDNEY • AUCKLAND

Today, Maisy and her friends are going on a nature walk.

Maisy packs her bag.

Hooray – all ready to go!

Everybody meets at the park entrance.
"I'm so excited!" says Tallulah.

"Me too!" agrees Maisy.

First, they visit the pond.

There are so many animals and plants living here!

Quack Quack

Charley crouches down for a closer look.

Ribbit Ribbit

"Hello, tadpoles! Hello, fish!
Hello, dragonfly!"

The animals who live in
the woods are very shy.
Who can you see?

There are chirping noises up in the trees!

Cheep Cheep

Maisy spots a bird and her chicks.

Tweet
Tweet

Maisy looks for minibeasts hiding under logs and in the leaves. The ants are very busy!

The next stop is the wildflower garden. What's that buzzing sound?

The bees are busy making honey!

Buzz Buzz Buzz

Using a magnifying glass, Cyril looks at the tiny creatures living by the flowers.

Eddie finds the perfect tree to build a den!

Maisy and Cyril collect little twigs.

Charley looks
for branches
and sticks.

Tallulah picks
daisies for
a special
surprise.

What a marvellous den!

"Surprise!" says Tallulah. She has made everyone lovely flower crowns.

"Thank you, Tallulah!"

What a wonderful day
exploring outside.
"I love the park!"
says Maisy.